© 2010 by Parragon Books Ltd

This 2010 edition published by Sandy Creek,
by arrangement with Parragon.

Sandy Creek
122 Fifth Avenue
New York, NY 10011

ISBN-13: 978-1-4351-2357-1

Printed and bound in China

1 3 5 7 9 10 8 6 4 2

101 DALMATIANS

My story begins in London, where I lived with my pet, Roger Radcliff. Roger was a songwriter and we lived in a bachelor apartment near Regent's Park. My name is Pongo. I'm the one with the spots, looking out the window.

As far as I could see, a bachelor's life was downright dull. So when I saw the perfect dog walk by with a lovely lady, it was a dream come true.

I grabbed my leash and barked loudly, "Rrrruff, rrrruff!" Roger understood and took me out.

As I pulled Roger along, he asked me, "Pongo, old boy. What's the hurry?"

Then I spotted the lovely Dalmatian and her pet. I slowed down as we walked by, hoping we'd catch their eye.

But when I looked back, they were starting to leave. Thinking fast, I wrapped up Roger and the lovely lady in my leash.

"Ohhhhh! Ohhh dear!" they cried, losing their balance and falling right into a pond. After a moment, they couldn't help but laugh. My plan had worked!

Not long after that, Anita and Roger were married.

And I took Perdita to be my bride.

For the first six months, we lived in a small house near the park. It was perfect for two couples just starting out. We even had a wonderful housekeeper named Nanny.

I thought that we couldn't be any happier, but Perdita had the best news yet!

"Oh, Pongo, we're going to have puppies," she announced happily one day.

One day an old classmate of Anita's, Cruella De Vil, stopped by. "Darling," she asked Anita, "where are the little brutes . . . er, puppies?"

"They won't be here for at least three weeks," replied Anita anxiously.

"Let me know when the Dalmatians arrive. Don't forget!" Cruella demanded.

On a stormy night three weeks later, Nanny cheered, "The puppies are here! All fifteen of them!" Then thunder cracked and Cruella swooped into the room.

"I'm here for the puppies—I'll buy them all!" Cruella sneered. She started to write a check, splattering ink everywhere.

"We're not selling the puppies and that's final!" shouted Roger.

Cruella stormed out.
"Perdy, don't worry. We're keeping the puppies,"
I whispered. "Every last one of them!" Perdita sighed
happily and we went to sleep.

Weeks passed, and our fifteen little ones certainly kept us busy! One of the things the puppies liked best was watching the adventures of Thunderbolt the dog on television.

"Bedtime, children," said Perdita when the show was over.
Nanny tucked the puppies in as we left for our nightly walk in
the park with Roger and Anita.

Just as Nanny had lulled the little ones off to sleep, the doorbell rang.

Two men, Jasper and Horace, were at the door. "We're here to inspect the . . . uhh . . . wiring," said Jasper. Then the two pushed their way into the house.

"You're not comin' in here!" shouted Nanny. "I'll call the police!"
But before she could do anything, they locked her in her room.
When Nanny finally escaped, she made a terrible discovery. The
puppy basket was empty!

I knew that Cruella must have chuckled when she read the morning's newspaper headline: FIFTEEN PUPPIES STOLEN—THIEVES FLEE. Her plan had worked!

That evening in the park, I said to Perdita, "It's up to us to find the puppies." We decided to use the Twilight Bark, an all-dog alert. I barked as loudly as I could.

The news traveled quickly out to the country, where a bloodhound named Towser heard the shocking story.

"Ruff! Ruff!" he barked, trying to reach the Colonel, an English sheepdog that lived nearby.

Towser's message reached the Colonel and his friends.

Then Sergeant Tibs the cat said, "I heard puppies barking at the old De Vil place two nights ago."

The friends decided to investigate the mansion. Sergeant Tibs sneaked through a hole in the wall and found a room . . . overflowing with Dalmatian puppies!

The fifteen missing puppies were there, but they weren't alone. Jasper and Horace had brought a total of ninety-nine puppies to the house!

Sergeant Tibs hid when he heard Cruella arrive. She screamed at Jasper and Horace, "I don't care how you kill the spotted beasties! I want my coats tonight!" Then she stormed out to her car and sped away.

Sergeant Tibs couldn't believe his ears. Cruella
wanted the puppies for fur coats!

There was no time to lose. He quickly helped the
puppies to escape from the room through the hole
in the wall.

Suddenly Horace and Jasper noticed that the puppies were missing.

"Follow me!" cried Sergeant Tibs, hiding the pups beneath the staircase.

Horace and Jasper ran after them calling, "Here, puppies. Here, puppies."

Meanwhile, Perdita and I had sneaked out of our house. Thanks to the dogs in London, we heard what had happened and began our journey to the De Vil mansion.

When we arrived at last, we found the Colonel standing in front of the gate.

"Follow me," he said, heading to the house. "I'm afraid there's trouble! Big hullabaloo!"

Through the window, we saw that Horace and Jasper had cornered the puppies.

Perdita and I broke through the glass with a crash and surprised the evil men. Those dognappers were no match for us!

We gathered the puppies and escaped from the mansion to a nearby barn. But we didn't realize that Jasper and Horace were hot on our trail!

In the barn, we counted up all the puppies. There were ninety-nine! Without hesitating I said, "We'll take them all home with us. Every last one of them."

Suddenly we heard a truck screech outside. It was Horace and Jasper! "You'd better go!" said the Colonel. "I'll stay behind to fend them off."

"Come on, kids, hurry!" cried Perdita as we made our escape into the snowy night.

The thieves escaped from the Colonel and Sergeant Tibs and followed our tracks in the snow. Sliding across an icy creek, we hid beneath a bridge. Finally, they drove off.

Our long journey continued. Just when we thought we couldn't take another step, we ran into a helpful collie. "We have shelter for you at a dairy farm," he said.

At the barn, four cows offered our grateful puppies warm milk, and the collie was kind enough to bring Perdy and me scraps to eat. Worn out, we slept soundly that night.

In the morning, we rounded up our puppies and headed for Dinsford, where a Labrador was waiting to help us.

As we ducked beneath a fence and crossed a road, I heard a car horn honking in the distance. "Hurry, kids! Hurry!" I said, shooing them along.

Cruella's car came roaring up the road. She screeched to a halt near our tracks in the snow.

Jasper and Horace pulled up next to her in their truck.

Cruella cried, "Their tracks are heading for the village. I'll take the main road, you check the side roads."

At Dinsford, the black Labrador announced that he had found us a ride to London! While we waited in a blacksmith's shop, I came up with a clever disguise to fool Cruella.

"Come on, kids," I ordered them. "Roll in the ashes!" Soon we all looked like black Labradors!

When our ride was ready, we began leading the disguised puppies out to the truck. Cruella and her henchmen didn't even glance our way.

But as we were helping the last little ones onto the truck, some melted snow fell on one of the pups. His spotted coat was revealed!

Cruella yelled, "There they go!"

Our truck sped off and Cruella raced after us, smashing into us at every turn. She was trying to force us off the cliff!

Then Horace and Jasper's truck came speeding toward us from the other direction. Our driver quickly swerved out of the way, and Cruella's car crashed into Horace and Jasper's truck. The three villains tumbled down the cliff and into a snowbank.

At long last, we made it back to London. Roger and Anita
hugged and cleaned us as we walked through the door.
We were all so happy to be together again!

As Nanny cleaned off our puppies, she giggled, "Oh, they're all here, the little dears!" That was when she noticed there were many, many more of us.

"Look!" Nanny cried joyously. "There are a whole lot more puppies!" Yes, indeed, there were.

When they had finished counting us, Roger said in amazement,
"There are a hundred and one Dalmatians! Let's buy a big place
in the country and have a . . . Dalmatian Plantation!"

The End